Tiger
deep-sea diver

T0372146

Lesley Sims

Illustrated by David Semple

She checks her map.
They're off to find
THE DRAGON OF THE DEEP!

Tiger's Diving Map

Dragon Rock

Old wreck

The Lost City

X

The boat is bobbing out at sea.
Rhino's on the deck.

It drifts away
past waving weed.
"The dragon!" Tiger thinks.

They chase it through a sunken town.

Oh no! It's just squid ink...

They climb back on the boat.

No luck?

Tiger frowns and shrugs.

The sub sinks down.

They sink some more. It's colder now.
They're in the midnight zone.

"Let's go deeper," Tiger begs.
"The dragon could be near."

"It's amazing!" Chimp shouts out.
"But there's no dragon here."

They reach the seabed. Tiger sighs.
"We've really had no luck."

"But think of what we've seen,"
Chimp cries.

"Time to go back up."

"Did you find it?" Rhino calls.
Tiger shakes her head.

Tiger fills an empty tank...

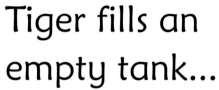

...with water from the sea.

Starting to read

Even before children start to recognize words, they can learn about the pleasures of reading. Encouraging a love of stories and a joy in language is the best place to start.

About phonics

When children learn to read in school, they are often taught to recognize words through phonics. This teaches them to identify the sounds of letters that are then put together to make words. An important first step is for children to hear rhymes, which help them to listen out for the sounds in words.

You can find out more about phonics on the Usborne website at **usborne.com/Phonics**

Phonics Readers

These rhyming books provide the perfect combination of fun and phonics. They are lively and entertaining with great storylines and quirky illustrations. They have the added bonus of focusing on certain sounds so in this story your child will soon identify the long *i* sound, as in **Tiger** and **diver.** Look out, too, for rhymes such as **dark – shark** and **near – here**.

Reading with your child

If your child is reading a story to you, don't rush to correct mistakes, but be ready to prompt or guide if needed. Above all, give plenty of praise and encouragement.

Edited by Jenny Tyler
Designed by Sam Whibley
Reading consultants: Alison Kelly and Anne Washtell

First published in 2024 by Usborne Publishing Limited, 83-85 Saffron Hill, London EC1N 8RT, United Kingdom. usborne.com Copyright © 2024 Usborne Publishing Limited. The name Usborne and the Balloon logo are registered trade marks of Usborne Publishing Limited. All rights reserved. No part of this publication may be reproduced, stored in a retrieval system or transmitted in any form or by any means without prior permission of the publisher. UE.